From Sour to Sweet
With Mr. Lemonsworth

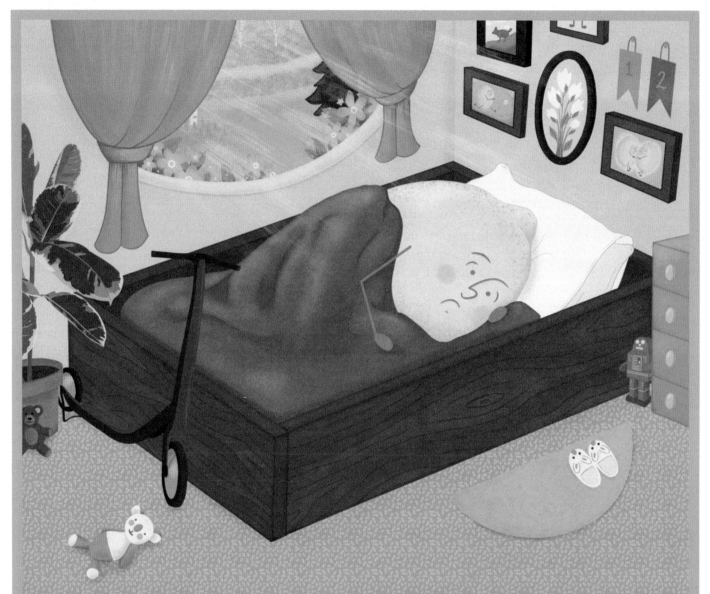

Mr. Lemonsworth woke up grumpy this morning. He was a lemon, after all. But even though he was a lemon, he didn't like feeling so sour.

He knew what would make him feel better — a cup of hot tea! So Mr. Lemonsworth made his messy bed, stepped into his slippers, and cruised into the kitchen to start the kettle.

Mr. Lemonsworth enjoyed the flavors of honey and cinnamon as he slowly sipped his tea. He felt calm and cozy as the sour feeling started to slightly slip away.

"A stroll along the stream will do me some good,"
he thought. So, Mr. Lemonsworth cleaned out his cup,
tidied his tea, and bounced into his boots.

"The stream is so lovely,"
He said aloud as he began his walk.

He felt a pep in his step as he enjoyed the greens of the grass, the browns of the branches, and the blues of the birds.

Amongst the chirping of the birds, he heard a sound.
It was not a happy sound, but a sad sort of sniffling sound.

It was Ms. Katie Pillar, sobbing on the opposite side of the stream. "Why are you so sad Ms. Katie Pillar?" asked Mr. Lemonsworth.

"I feel frustrated," she responded. "I need to cross the stream, but the bridge has washed away. How will I get across?"

Mr. Lemonsworth did not like seeing Ms. Katie Pillar feeling so sour. He knew there had to be a way to help.

Surrounding them was the scent of spring flowers, which gave Mr. Lemonsworth an idea.

He picked a few flowers, tied them together,
and threw one end across the stream.

Ms. Katie Pillar tied her end to a rock. Then, they gave the knot a tug to test that it was tight.

She took a deep breath and wobbled across the flowers, over the water.

"We did it!" they exclaimed. It gave them so much joy to solve a problem together. For a moment, Mr. Lemonsworth didn't feel sour at all!

Mr. Lemonsworth invited Ms. Katie Pillar to join him on his walk. He loved the idea of sharing the sights and sounds of the stream with his newfound friend.

It felt only natural to whistle along with the squeaking of the squirrels, the buzzing of the bees, and the fluttering of the butterflies.

Amongst their own melody, they heard a sound. It was not a happy sound, but a sad sort of sniffling sound.

It was Sir Snailton, crying in the middle of the stream. "Why are you so sad, Sir Snailton?" asked Mr. Lemonsworth.

"I feel frightened," he responded. "I was nibbling on this lovely leaf and slipped into the stream. How will I get back to shore?"

They didn't like seeing Sir Snailton feeling so sour. They knew there had to be a way to help.

Surrounding them was the sound of twirling twigs
in the breeze, and that gave Ms. Katie Pillar an idea.

She picked up a long twig and held it out far enough to reach Sir Snailton. He took hold of the twig and held on tight.

Mr. Lemonsworth and Ms. Katie Pillar took a deep breath as they pulled Sir Snailton to shore.

"Thank you my friends!" exclaimed Sir Snailton.
It gave them so much joy to solve a problem together.

"This has been quite the day," said Mr. Lemonsworth. "Would you both like to join me for a cup of tea?"

"Yes please," Ms. Katie Pillar replied happily.

"Tea sounds terrific," said Sir Snailton.

The three of them smiled as they made their way back to the home of Mr. Lemonsworth.

He showed them the perfect place to sit on his porch,
then went into the kitchen to make three cups of hot tea.

Everyone enjoyed the flavors of honey and cinnamon as they slowly sipped. No one heard an unhappy sound, a sad sort of sniffling sound.

But they knew if they did, they would be able to help.
They would solve the problem together. This made
them feel sweet, not sour at all.